WA 1314283 6

REAL-TIME REPORTING

By John Hamilton

VISIT US AT
WWW.ABDOPUB.COM

Published by ABDO & Daughters, an imprint of ABDO Publishing Company, 4940 Viking Drive, Suite 622, Edina, Minnesota 55435.

Printed in the United States.

Edited by: Tamara L. Britton and Kate A. Conley
Graphic Design: Arturo Leyva, David Bullen
Cover Design: Castaneda Dunham, Inc.
Photos: AP/Wide World, Corbis, Library of Congress

Learning Resources
Centre

13142836

Library of Congress Cataloging-in-Publication Data

Hamilton, John, 1959-
    Real-time reporting / John Hamilton.
       p. cm. -- (War in Iraq)
    Includes bibliographical references (p.) and index.
    Summary: Discusses some of the advantages and disadvantages of the real-time reporting of the 2003 Iraq War and provides some background on the history of war correspondents.
    ISBN 1-59197-497-6
    1. Iraq War, 2003--Juvenile literature. [1. Iraq War, 2003. 2. War correspondents. 3. Journalism.] I. Title. II. Series.

    DS79.763.H36 2003
    070.4'4995670443--dc22

                    2003052305

TABLE OF CONTENTS

News coverage shows images of a Saddam Hussein statue falling in Baghdad.

THE NEW LIVING ROOM WAR

One week into Operation Iraqi Freedom, the American public saw more of the conflict than they saw in all of 1991's Persian Gulf War. New technology had created a real-time television war. Americans were able to tune in any time of the day to see behind-the-scenes images and breathless reports from journalists riding alongside U.S. combat troops. U.S. defense secretary Donald Rumsfeld noted that the coverage Americans saw was historic. "We're having a conflict at a time in our history," he said, "when we have 24-hours-a-day television, radio, media and Internet and more people in the world have access to what is taking place."

This amazing access to raw information, however, came at a price. Sometimes snippets of news could be taken out of context, making the big picture jumbled and confused. Worse, in the frenzy of war, news could be manipulated for political purposes by both sides of the conflict. For example, many Americans believed that the Arabic television network

6

al-Jazeera gave a decidedly anti-American slant to its war coverage. At the same time, many people thought that American news networks were equally biased toward the U.S. war effort.

Despite this, Americans turned to the media for on-the-spot news reports from the front lines. These reports gave viewers a better feel for what individual soldiers endured in combat. In addition, the Pentagon's new system of embedding more than 500 media personnel into coalition combat units put a human face on the war. Many viewers felt more patriotic after watching such news reports. They were proud to support the brave troops. This is exactly what the military had hoped to gain by letting reporters have open access to the battlefield.

On the other hand, some people criticized the news coverage for failing to provide enough context and background. What was the overall war strategy? What was the coalition aiming to accomplish and why? How was this war fought differently from other wars? Many thought the press should have questioned President George W. Bush's administration more closely on its claim that the regime of Saddam Hussein possessed weapons of mass destruction. By being embedded with the military, was the press too quick to take the Pentagon's word for everything that happened on the battlefield?

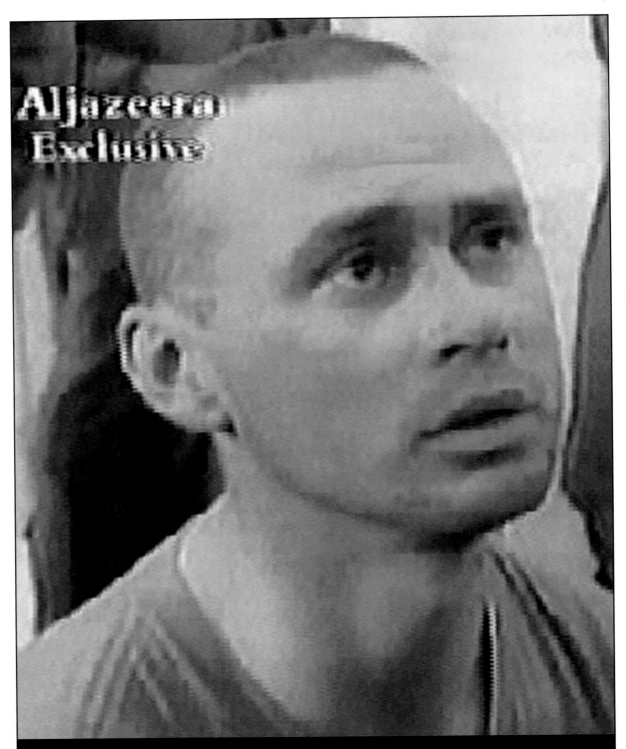

Prisoner of War Sergeant James Riley is interviewed on Iraqi television.

From the government's point of view, press coverage worked well for the most part. After a week of combat, however, the government discovered that its open-access policy had downsides, too. Images of dead Americans, plus U.S. soldiers taken prisoner by Iraq and paraded on television, hurt the morale of the troops and the public alike. Inaccurate reports from the battlefield added to the confusion.

The phrase *fog of war* refers to the confusion that surrounds all wars. Nobody is 100 percent sure of what is happening at any particular moment on the battlefield. This includes U.S. commanders, despite the information they receive from special forces troops and high-flying Predator drones. Journalists, of course, have even less information at their fingertips. They have to report what they see at the moment, unfiltered, and often out of context. The big question is, did today's real-time reporting help our understanding of what really happened in the war with Iraq?

HISTORY OF WAR REPORTING

"In war, truth is the first casualty."
Aeschylus, ancient Greek dramatist

During wartime, governments will usually try to manipulate the media, hoping for positive news and trying to silence battlefield disappointments. Similarly, misinformation is also used to confuse the enemy, or to draw attention away from a scandal or mishap. This kind of propaganda is common, even in the United States, where the First Amendment guarantees a free and open press.

Despite this, the duty of a free and open press is to scrutinize all sides of an issue, even if the public doesn't like what it reads and sees. In some countries, the government owns and operates the media. This makes it easier for the government to control what information its people receive. A free and open press, however, allows the people of free democracies to tell whether their governments are working in their best interests.

The goal of a journalist is to be as impartial as possible when reporting the news. However, journalists are human beings, and their stories are colored by their backgrounds. This dilemma has proven particularly difficult during wartime. For example, during the American Civil War (1861-1865), the stories were often biased depending on whether the reporter came from the North or the South.

Despite this bias, the American public had a huge appetite for news during this period. New technology fostered this interest. Mathew Brady used photography to document the drama and horror of war for the first time in history. And Samuel F.B. Morse's telegraph solved the problem of long-distance communication, allowing reports from the battlefield to be read the very next day.

So for the first time in U.S. history, journalists were sent to the front lines. This new kind of journalist was called the war correspondent. These reporters risked their lives to bring back news of the war. The North had more than 500 reporters covering the war, while the South had about 100 correspondents. Never before had the public been so well informed. However, the governments of both sides severely restricted reporters' access to the battlefield. It was a classic case of the public's right to know versus the military's need for secrecy. Faced with

House by a Vote of 373 to 50 Passes Joint Resolution

WAR IS DECLARED BY U. S.

Interned German Ships Seized by Customs Authorities

Washington, April 6.—After a debate of nearly seventeen hours, the House early to-day passed the resolution previously adopted in the Senate, declaring a state of war against the Government of Germany. The vote was 373 to 50.

The resolution now goes to Vice-President Marshall, who must sign it in formal session of the Senate. It will then be taken before the President for his signature.

Amendments to prevent the use of United States military forces in Europe, Asia or Africa unless directed by Congress were voted down. The resolution adopted by the Senate on Wednesday was approved by the House without the crossing of a "t" or the dotting of an "i."

VESSELS IN PORT HERE TAKEN

U. S. in Possession of Teuton Boats Moored in North River.

Within an hour of the passage by the House of the war resolution, United States Customs officials had taken possession of three of the German ships moored in the Hudson off. One Hundred and Thirty-fifth street. They are the Prinz Eitel Friedrich, the Allemania and the Hamburg.

It was expected that the other ships lying nearby, the Prinz Joachim and Koenig Wilhelm II, would also be seized, as well as the German vessels interned at Hoboken.

A report was received early to-day from the effect that five German steamships, which have been of refuge on that port, were ordered seized, and their crews dispossessed.

MALONE ACTS.

Dudley Field Malone, Collector of the Port of New York, following a hurried visit to Washington where he conferred with President Wilson and Secretary of the Treasury McAdoo, has ordered every man in the custom service to report at the Customs House prepared to move the 1,550 officers and men from the German vessels to the port the moment war is declared.

As soon as the result of the war vote in the House was announced the ship plans into operation.

German officers and sailors aboard the interned liners in Hoboken, including the great Vaterland, were told and deemed ready for whatever might be commanded of them. Seven officers thought the ships would be seized; others that, as German laws require to be held involuntarily in the Government. Over the fact that the machinery of all the ships has been damaged so that none now are navigable, there was unconcealed satisfaction.

Government tugs aided in moving the Main and the German sailing vessels, which have been at anchor of Ellis Island since the beginning of the war, across the bay to

continued on Page 2, Column 4.

ALLIES REST BEFORE BIG DRIVE

Prepare for Final Smash at St. Quentin—French Recover Aisne Ground.

London, April 6.—French and British troops are preparing to-day for the final attack on St. Quentin. That it will be a stubborn struggle is borne out by reports of patrols and by the fierceness with which the Germans yesterday attempted a new attack to drive back the Allies.

The bitterest fighting of the past twenty-four hours has developed to the south of the Hindenburg line, along the left bank of the Aisne Canal, where the Germans precipitated a fierce battle.

Their object was to clear the French from the north bank. Picked troops attacked on a front of a mile and a half between Bagneux and Chivres farm, and the impetuosity of the onset yielded a temporary success.

FRENCH RETAKE TRENCHES.

French War Office report says the French almost immediately re-occupied the greater part of the first line trenches the Germans had captured. Counter attacks, it adds, are progressing against some elements still held by the Germans.

The German official communiqué of to-day, as received here, claims the Germans inflicted an sanguinary reverse on the French in an elaborately prepared and vigorously executed undertaking north of Rheims.

Eight hundred men were made prisoners, the communication says.

Further north, on the firing line French reconnoitering parties advanced last night north of Gauchy and May, in the region of St. Quentin, until they reached new German lines, which they found to be occupied strongly. Artillery fighting is in progress over the front between Laffaux and Maroilval.

The British have added two more villages to their holdings in the sector northeast of Peronne, the British War Office reports. These are Penneay and Bann—Baisigne. In the St. Quentin district no important change is noted. The "capture of the two villages named carries the British within two and three-quarter miles of the St. Quentin-Cambrai road, about nine miles north of St. Quentin.

"LOVE U. S. BUT CAN'T VOTE FOR WAR"---MISS RANKIN

PHOTO © INTERNATIONAL

MISS JEANETTE RANKIN.

Washington, April 6.—In the midst of the roll call, while the House sat in solemn silence listening to the responses, the name of Miss Jeanette Rankin, the first woman to sit in the House, was called. In the rear of the hall a little black-clad figure arose, and a thin voice, quivering with emotion, sobbed out:

"I want to stand for my country, but I cannot vote for war."

The little figure swayed and two of her colleagues half-led, half-carried the weeping form of the first Congresswoman from the chamber.

Her vote was recorded against the resolution.

CZAR SUPPLIANT FOR PENSION TO DUMA

Petrograd, April 6.—Once Czar of all the Russians and probably the wealthiest man of all the world, Nicholas Romanoff to-day is a suppliant for subsistence before the government that dethroned him. A request has been made to the Russian Duma for a pension to care for him and his family.

As attempts for regaining the throne may be expected.

The Romanoffs are likely to be no more possessors of those whose wealth they spent once with a lavish, wasted and notorious profligacy.

Russian soldiers allowed to-day that the revolution has not demoralized their fighting powers. The Textons attacked sometimes a single small part of the Russian front in northern Galicia, but the Russians held the positions as activly as they were before the first attack.

CARRANZISTAS MASSING ON BORDER

El Paso, April 5.—De facto troops in the United States of Nuevo Laredo, Coahuila and Chihuahua have begun a general movement toward the American border, according to highly reliable information received here to-night.

The movement in these three border States has been officially reported to Washington and is being watched closely.

In Chihuahua a movement is being made in a northwesterly direction by General Murguia's troops. The reason given by Carranza officials is that it is an offensive campaign against Villa.

Washington, April 6.—The War Department's comprehensive border reports show no indication of a general northward movement of Mexican troops. Officials have no fear of an attempt at invasion.

Recent investigations have shown army officers say, that the Mexicans in that section are too poorly organized and equipped to do serious damage.

Drives Stolen Car in Path of Owner

Detroit, Mich., April 6.— When Everett Gilbert, about thirty years old, who gave his address as No. 49 Cherry street, took an automobile owned by William L. March, manager of the Browne Carburetor Co. offices in the David Whitney building, he drove in the wrong direction.

While Mr. March was seated in a friend's motor car at Woodward and Adams avenues last Saturday afternoon March's machine whizzed past. March and his friend gave chase and with the assistance of Patrolman Albert J. Henderson, overtook the machine and arrested Gilbert.

Held at Asbury Park for Murder in Indiana

Asbury Park, N. J., April 6.—Andrew H. Seagen, a Russian, was arrested at a hotel here by County Detective T. J. McCormack, at the instance of the authorities of Fort Wayne, Ind. Seagen is wanted there in connection with the death of his companion, George Johnson. Seagen is said to have collected the insurance on Johnson's life. Subsequently it was found that Johnson died from poison.

Seagen admitted he came from Fort Wayne, but denied causing the death of Johnson.

President's Historic Address Free to Journal Readers

President Wilson's historic address to Congress is now accessible to New York Evening Journal readers in permanent form, free of cost. Beginning to-day, a large, finely decorated copy, suitable for framing, may be obtained by each general movement toward the American border, according to highly reliable information received here to-night.

Manhattan—No. 2 Columbus Circle; or No. 238 William street (seventh floor). Brooklyn—No. 298 Washington street.

Printed on calendered paper, the document is surmounted by a picture of the President and the American flag in colors.

B. F. McCarton, Jr., Actor.

Benjamin F. McCarton, Jr., thirty-eight years old, known on the stage as Frank Carlot, died from a complication of ailments, at his residence, No. 365 Flatbush avenue, Brooklyn. Mr. McCarton was born in Philadelphia and was a play writer and actor.

AUSTRIA EAGER TO KEEP PEACE WITH U. S.

Copenhagen, April 6.—The expectation that Austria-Hungary and Turkey will remain neutral for the present at least in the conflict of Germany with the United States, prevails to-day in diplomatic circles here.

From dispassionate sources it is learned that such is the intention and desire of the two Governments, if left to themselves, but that if Germany insists on their making alliance their common cause with the senior partner in the alliance they will have to yield and formally declare war.

The desire to avoid a complete rupture with the United States is inspired not only by the wish to keep open the door to friendly relations after the war, but it is thought also that they may be able to act as mediators between Germany and the United States at some later period.

The Austrian Minister, Count Szechenyi, called to-day on the United States Minister, Maurice F. Egan, and friendly relations have been maintained by the Turkish Legation.

Corset Hurts Women's Brains, Is Charge

Long Beach, Cal., April 6.—Corsets and high heels are largely responsible for the "inferior physical and effinous mental quality of women," according to Dr A. C. Selberg, in an address before the Chamber of Commerce here. The physician said the manufacture of shoes and corsets should be regulated by the Legislature.

While the final vote was in progress a tense crowd watched from the galleries. spectacle was one of the most remarkable, the event certainly the most momentous, in the tory of the nation.

The discussion was characterized by many sensations. At one time the presiding officer of the House was compelled to direct the Sergeant-at-Arms to employ the official in enforcing the rules. There was a great deal of tumult, many spirited passages of words—almost fists—at stages of the debate.

It was understood early to-day that the moment the war resolution is signed the Government will take steps to place armed guards on the various German merchant ships which have found refuge at New York and other American ports since the outbreak of the war, and will probably take over the interned German war vessels in the American ports.

While no attempt is to be made to place unoffending persons of German nationality in concentration camps, the Secret Service agents of the Government, it is understood, will keep under surveillance hundreds of suspected spies in various parts of the country.

The action of the House, followed by the actual declaration of war by the President later to-day, was early seen as inevitable.

Before the House met it was freely predicted that a mere handful of Representatives would vote against the war resolution, after a speech by Representative Claude Kitchin, of North Carolina, the Democratic floor leader, in which he argued against the measure, there was seeming voting against the proposed measure, there was seemingly marked change among the contingent which had been wavering between the two sides of the controversy.

FIFTY WHO VOTED NO.

The fifty Representatives who voted against the resolution follow: Mason, Britten, Burnett, Cary, Church, Cooper, Kansas, Cooper of Wisconsin, Davis, Decker, Dill, Dillon, Esch, Evans, Fuller of Illinois, Haugen, Hayes of California, Hensley, Hull of Iowa, Johnson of South Dakota, King, Kinkaid of Nebraska, Knutson, La Follette, Little, Londres, McLemore, Mason, Randall, Miss Rankin, Reavis, Rodenberg, Shackleford, Sloan, Stafford, Van Dyke, Voigt, Wheeler and Woods of Iowa.

Speaker Champ Clark did not vote. As soon as the House had passed

MALONE ACTS. section continued

Auto Crushes Boy's Foot.

Four-year-old Walter Stankevich, of No. 296 South First street, Williamsburg, was struck by an auto near his home to-day. Jacob Cohen, of No. 334 Grand street, the driver, took him to Eastern District Hospital. The child's left foot was crushed.

Adeline Harper Dodge.

Mrs. Adeline Harper Dodge, widow of J. Edwin Dodge and a member of the Harper family of publishers, is dead to-day at her home, No. 107 Waverly place, in her fifty-ninth year.

such restrictions, and under intense pressure to get the story before their competition, many journalists filed inaccurate reports, or simply made up false battles in which their side won. So the press release was invented during the Civil War. The military gave reporters fact sheets that stated what they wanted the public to know.

During World War I (1914-1918), Congress passed laws that severely restricted how the press could cover the war. Laws such as the Espionage Act and the Sedition Act made it a crime to publish anything that the government decided would help the enemy. Many newspapers, especially German-language newspapers, were banned.

In addition, journalists could be jailed because of the Sedition Act, which made it a crime to write or publish ". . . any disloyal, profane, scurrilous or abusive language about the form of government of the United States or the Constitution of the United States, military or naval forces of the United States, flag of the United States or the uniform . . ." The law was written so broadly that the government could jail anyone writing anything bad about the war.

Covering World War I was an almost impossible job for American reporters. They were allowed to go to the front lines, but they were heavily censored by the military and their

Committee on Public Information (CPI)

This committee was created by Woodrow Wilson on April 13, 1917. It was led by a journalist named George Creel. Using advertising, big business, art, and journalism, the CPI was the largest propaganda movement in the history of the American government. Its news department handed out more than 6,000 press releases during World War I. Work produced by the CPI reached nearly 12 million people every month.

Woodrow Wilson

The CPI also helped pass the Espionage Act of 1917 and the Sedition Act of 1918. The committee also had a division in Hollywood called the Division of Films. It worked to promote the war through movies.

Franklin D. Roosevelt

Office of Censorship

This office was first created by Franklin D. Roosevelt during World War II. Its director was journalist Byron Price. The office had the "absolute discretion" to censor any overseas communications it thought necessary. The office employed more than 10,000 censors who routinely monitored magazines, mail, movies, newspapers, and radio broadcasts. Price believed that the goal of the organization should not be to tell media outlets what messages to run. Instead, he thought it was important to convince them to run positive American messages. His goal was to get the press to ask itself: "Is this information I would like to have if I were the enemy?"

newspapers. When the war began, British, French, and German soldiers were ordered to arrest any correspondent at the front. The British only had two official photographers working on the battlefield. Anyone else caught taking photos could be sent to a firing squad. American reporters took many photos and shot thousands of feet of motion-picture film, but censors didn't let the public see any of it until after the war. The government also controlled the airwaves, banning the use of wireless telegraphs. The transatlantic cable from England was heavily censored.

During World War I, President Woodrow Wilson created the Committee on Public Information (CPI), which was the first U.S. propaganda office. One of the CPI's goals was to flood newspapers with stories that would persuade the public to support the war. Most newspapers cooperated with the CPI and printed their press releases. During the war years, more than 6,000 CPI press releases ran in 118,000 daily newspapers. The public believed it was reading independent news coverage, when in fact it was receiving heavily censored and manipulated reports. After the war, the CPI was dissolved.

During World War II (1939-1945), the government relied on the self-censorship of news organizations. In 1941 and 1942, President Franklin D. Roosevelt created the Office of

Censorship and the Office of War Information. They monitored mail and radio communications between the United States and other countries. The Code of Wartime Practices for the American Press was issued on January 15, 1942. It told news organizations the government-approved way to report war news.

Censorship was extensive during World War II, but not as widespread as in the previous war. Broadcast journalism came of age during WWII. Many people turned to radio reports to learn the latest news and hear the sounds of war. Combat footage was played in newsreels at movie theaters. Newsreels showed life on the battlefield and put a human face on the war, unlike the heavily censored footage of World War I.

During the Korean War (1950-1953), the U.S. government once more turned to heavy censorship of news reports. The military expected the press to practice self-censorship. It handed out rules for what was considered acceptable reporting. Violators could be deported, or even court-martialed. As the Cold War began, it was considered unpatriotic to question a war against a communist country such as North Korea.

Reporting on the Korean War brought many challenges. Simply getting news out of the country was difficult. There were no darkrooms for the press to use in South Korea, so film

REAL-TIME REPORTING

After visiting the front lines, reporters from the *New York Herald Tribune* file stories regarding the Korean War.

had to be sent to Japan for processing. On the other hand, the press had very free access to the battlefield. The stories they brought to their readers—assuming the stories made it past the censors—were limited only by the risks they were willing to take.

In the Vietnam War (1957-1975), the rules of reporting changed again. At first, the military tried to dictate rules and regulations to control the media. But the rules were phased out or ignored because new communications technology limited military censorship in the field. At the beginning of the war, correspondents were frustrated by their own newspapers and television stations. That's because most of the newspapers and television stations fully supported the war and edited or ignored their correspondents' reports. After the Tet Offensive in 1968, however, the surprising success of the enemy shocked most media. They realized that the reports given by the military were too optimistic, and they didn't tell the whole story of what was happening in the war.

Most reports after 1968 were critical of the Vietnam War. The press blamed the military for misleading the public. On the other hand, the military blamed the press for negative coverage that it believed encouraged the public to be against the conflict. Some pointed to misleading television and photo

coverage. For example, Eddie Adams won the Pulitzer Prize for his 1968 photograph of a Vietcong suspect being executed by a South Vietnamese general. The photo shows a small, cringing man, in handcuffs, just before he is shot point-blank in the head. The photo became one of the defining points in the war, highlighting its cruelty and hopelessness. What the photo didn't show, however, was that the executed man had killed a police officer, his wife, and six children shortly before the photo was taken.

Reporters in Vietnam had much easier access to the battlefield than in previous wars. Reporters and photographers seemed to be everywhere, often arriving in combat zones by military transport. After getting their stories, they flew back to South Vietnam's capital, Saigon, and filed their reports back to the United States. Portable 16mm film cameras allowed television reporters to go anywhere in the country. Footage could be shot, flown to the United States, edited, and shown on television within 48 hours. At the height of the war, there were more than 100 million television sets in the United States. Because of extensive television coverage, the war in Vietnam was dubbed the Living Room War.

The U.S. military tried to give its version of how the Vietnam War was progressing by giving daily press briefings.

Press photographers dressed in military fatigues capture images of the Persian Gulf War.

However, these briefings were often outdated, inaccurate, or misleading. Many reporters had been on the battlefield and knew that the government was giving out bad information. The briefings became known as the Five O'clock Follies, and were widely ignored.

The U.S. military believed that reporting in Vietnam caused a loss of public support for the war effort. So all subsequent battlefields have been tightly controlled, with severe restrictions placed on the press.

During the 1991 Persian Gulf War, the military controlled almost all press access. Even though the press had high-tech tools to file up-to-the-minute reports, they were limited by where they could go. Reports were also censored, much like in World War II.

Desperate for news, in many cases the media simply repeated the stories told to them by the military. But sometimes the information was not entirely correct. In one example, the press believed that there was going to be an invasion of Iraq by sea. The press reported this information, and Saddam Hussein believed it, diverting several divisions of his army to defend the coast. In fact, the main attack came overland from the south and west, across the border with Kuwait. The misinformation worked for the U.S. military, but the danger for the press was that the public's confidence was eroded. Who knew what to believe?

In another example, confusion resulted over the success rate of weapons systems, especially of smart bombs and the high-tech Patriot missile, which is designed to shoot down enemy missiles. During one military briefing, General Norman Schwarzkopf said that 33 Iraqi Scud missiles were all shot down by Patriots. Later, President George H.W. Bush said 41 out of 42 Patriot missiles had shot down Scuds. After the war, two scientists at the Massachusetts Institute of Technology looked at the evidence and concluded that fewer than 10 percent of the Scuds had actually been intercepted. Schwarzkopf later commented on the issue saying, "you don't just make those things up. . . . If they have a choice one way or another . . . they're going to claim victory every time."

Despite the military's control of the media, some quality reporting was carried out during the Persian Gulf War. For example, in Baghdad, Bernard Shaw, John Holliman, and Peter Arnett gave live reports of the bombing of the Iraqi capital. Overall, however, journalists were severely hindered by poor battlefield access, censorship, and misinformation.

Even the military recognized that it was in their own best interests to make press coverage more free and open. The

LIVE

PETER ARNETT
NBC NEWS
NATIONAL GEOGRAPHIC EXPLOI
E IRAQIS   ABOUT 150 ANTI-W

Journalist Peter Arnett reports from Baghdad during Operation Iraqi Freedom.

press and the military had a better working relationship during the war in Bosnia/Kosovo in the 1990s, and during Operation Enduring Freedom in Afghanistan in 2001-2002. But the press was still restricted, and any freedom they enjoyed was due in large part to improved communications technology, which made it much more difficult for the military to censor reporters.

To keep at least partial control over the media, while at the same time loosening the rules of war reporting, the government decided to embed reporters right alongside combat troops. It was an idea that both sides eagerly pursued, and it would be used to a great extent in Operation Iraqi Freedom, the 2003 war in Iraq.

EMBEDDED REPORTERS

In Operation Iraqi Freedom, more than 500 reporters were embedded in U.S. military units. They ate, drank, and slept right alongside the troops. Commanders were warned not to keep reporters from the battlefield for personal safety reasons. That meant reporters could go anywhere and report on anything as long as they didn't give out operational secrets, such as telling the exact location of their units.

Embedding is a new system. It was developed after the Persian Gulf War, when the Pentagon received criticism for giving the press virtually no access to the battlefield. Members of the press had to take the military's word for what was happening. They received most of their information at daily press briefings far from the action. Some of that information later turned out to be false, but reporters had no way of verifying the information since they were kept away from the battlefield. News blackouts resulted in the public not knowing the truth until long after the war had ended.

War reporters faced the same dangers that troops encountered. Here, journalists take cover in Scud bunkers alongside U.S. and British troops.

Bryan Whitman, a spokesman for the U.S. Department of Defense and the chief planner of the embedding program, said that embedding journalists with combat troops increased the safety for both the reporters and the military. The bonus for reporters is that they have unprecedented access to the battlefield as the fighting occurs. Whitman's bosses at the Pentagon agreed to the arrangement. Besides, they reasoned, it would be almost impossible to enforce a blanket news blackout like the kind in the Persian Gulf War. That's because new technology, such as satellite phones and mobile Internet hookups, made censorship much more difficult.

The embedding system worked very well, according to almost everyone involved. Still, there were problems, not the least of which was the personal danger faced by reporters. Commanders in the field decided how close to the action reporters actually got. But commanders had other more important worries, such as fighting the enemy. So in many cases, embedded reporters made their own decisions on how near to the fighting they wished to be.

In small military units in the middle of a firefight, grave danger is always present. It was only a matter of time before reporters started getting hurt and killed. Whitman said, "We fully planned for this, even if our greatest hope was we wouldn't have any deaths. We knew reporters were getting in harm's way." One reporter confirmed that it was a very dangerous assignment. "It's getting hairier. You can hear the bullets whizzing by."

Embedded reporters brought an immediacy to the war that was lacking in previous conflicts. As a result, television networks that relied heavily on embeds saw their ratings skyrocket. The reports from the field made the war up close and personal to a public eager to hear how its troops were doing.

Kevin Peraino, reporting for *Newsweek*, was embedded with the U.S. Army's Third Infantry Division. He filed this report as U.S. troops raced across the desert toward Baghdad: "When Captain Todd (T.K.) Kelly crossed the border into Iraq, the moon had not yet risen. Thick dust clouds clung to the columns of tanks and Bradley fighting vehicles as they rumbled through the berm ahead of him."

Peraino reported that Kelly complained of not being able to see because of the dust kicked up by the armored vehicles. "Then a spectacular volley of U.S. artillery shells crashed down ahead of [Kelly], electrifying the desert night. 'Is that bright enough for you, sir?' one of Kelly's grunts deadpanned on the radio. The guys in the Bradley grabbed a few hours of sleep around 3 A.M. that night. The back of

Michael Kelly, editor and columnist for *The Atlantic*

the Bradley smelled like socks and armpits; dirty clothes were piled next to antitank missiles, stacks of M-16s and flak vests. They rolled down the ramp on the back of the Bradley and just went to sleep on the steel. Then they were up before dawn, moving again."

Peraino's exciting report gave readers back home a realistic glimpse of what war was like for the average soldier. In that sense, the embedding system worked. The military saw its troops portrayed in a mostly favorable light, and the networks enjoyed good ratings. The coverage was popular because the networks, working with the military, managed to put a human face on the war. In many ways it was a brilliant public relations move.

Another reason the military agreed to open up press access was to preserve the history of the war. Said reporter Michael Kelly, "There was a real sense after the last gulf war that witness had been lost. The people in the military care about that history a great deal, because it is their history. I think that is the primal motivating impulse here, and they decided to take a gamble."

The Pentagon's Bryan Whitman said, "We realized early on that our adversary was a practiced liar. What better way to mitigate the lies and deception of Saddam Hussein than having trained, objective observers out there in the field?"

On the other hand, many argue that the embed system made the war more difficult to understand for the average viewer. Some compare it to looking at an elephant through a drinking straw: you only get to see a small part of the larger picture. Even U.S. defense secretary Donald Rumsfeld said the embedded reporters were only showing small slices of the war. With this lack of overall context, many argue that the public was actually less informed. Images of U.S. tanks rolling across the desert, or of dust-covered reporters wearing flak vests, didn't necessarily mean the news coverage was timely or even accurate. Many complained that entertainment value had replaced hard news, especially in television reporting.

Journalist Bill Moyers, when asked about the impact of so many different media voices bombarding the American public, observed that, "For a professional journalist, it's media heaven. But for the typical citizen, it must be very confusing. . . . My impression is that the buildup to the war, and the first few weeks of the war, were all driven by the government's mission and the government's definition of what is news. . . . As the war has gone on and news has happened out there, we're

Former U.S. president Theodore Roosevelt

beginning to get more important pieces, pieces that are much at odds with the official view of reality."

Another problem with embedded reporters was the chance that they would bond with the troops they traveled with. This is natural, considering that the reporters and the troops faced life and death together. However, some question whether the bonding made the reporters biased. Many reported that they were uncomfortable portraying their comrades in an unfavorable light. They were made to feel unpatriotic if they criticized the war or President Bush.

Many years ago, President Theodore Roosevelt said, "To announce that there must be no criticism of the president is not only unpatriotic and servile, but is morally treasonable." Of course, President Roosevelt wasn't living in an age of satellite communications, smart bombs, and instant polls. Things are much more complex today. But the principles of a free press hold true. For the public to be well informed, reporters must be free to do their jobs. Carol Morello, a journalist working for the *Washington Post*, said, "If we can't cover the news, we become a public relations arm."

HIGH-TECH NEWS GATHERING

The most striking parts of the news coverage of Operation Iraqi Freedom were the real-time images that seemed to dominate the airwaves 24 hours a day. But television wasn't the only medium that saw increased use in covering the war. The Internet has also grown in importance in war reporting.

According to Nielsen/NetRatings, there are now 64.4 million broadband high-speed Internet connections in the United States. In addition, the percentage of Americans who use Net video or audio has nearly doubled, to 44 percent, since the year 2000, according to Arbitron's MeasureCast. The Internet can be used to send photos, video, and text very quickly to anyone in the world with a proper computer setup.

Many people received their war news by checking in with Web logs, or blogs. Blogs are on-line diaries created by groups or single individuals, often updated at least once a day. Most blogs aren't professionally created, but are done by interested

Pedestrians watch the latest news on the war in Iraq.

people who wish to express themselves, or gather news and post it for the whole world to see. Sometimes the information posted on blogs isn't accurate. But there is a sense of immediacy to blogs, a you-are-there feeling, that makes them appealing.

Over the course of the war, many blogs were created that gave day-to-day accounts of what soldiers went through during the conflict. Sometimes blogs beat traditional sources with up-to-the-minute news. They also encourage feedback, making them even more appealing to some readers. An anonymous person, writing under the name of Salam Pax, created one of the most interesting blogs, with reports from within the Iraqi capital of Baghdad. The blog contained riveting accounts of life during the U.S. bombing campaign. Because it originated on the Internet, where anonymity practically guarantees free speech, the blog was one of the very few journalistic accounts to come out of Iraq that wasn't heavily censored by the Iraqi government.

Even though the Internet was an important source of information for many people, the dominant media forms were still television, radio, and print journalism. Technology has evolved to a point where small teams of journalists can file their reports from almost anywhere in the world, in real time.

Digital camera images and digital video can be beamed immediately to newsrooms. Newspapers no longer have to wait for film to arrive and be processed. Instead, digital images can be transmitted from the war zone and sent directly to be laid out and printed.

The heart of this information revolution is satellite technology. In 1980, Ted Turner started the Cable News Network (CNN). A direct competitor to the network news channels, CNN was broadcast by satellite to nearly every country in the world, 24 hours a day. CNN had a major impact in the way news was delivered during the Persian Gulf War.

In addition to sending the news, satellites are also used to gather reports from the field. Small satellite uplinks convert video and audio signals into radio waves and send them to a satellite in space. The satellite bounces the signal to a satellite dish at the studio headquarters. From there the signal is converted back into video and audio, edited, and then put on the air for consumers. Instead of being partially dependent on the military to file their stories, journalists can now make direct contact with each other and their newsrooms.

The main newsroom in CNN headquarters in Atlanta, Georgia

A DANGEROUS PROFESSION

More than 700 journalists around the world have died covering war and conflict. During Operation Iraqi Freedom, more than a dozen names were added to this tragic list. Several were killed after being caught in the crossfire between coalition troops and Iraqi defenders. Others died from missile attacks and suicide bombings. With more than 500 reporters risking their lives alongside coalition forces, casualties were bound to occur.

In a solemn ceremony April 27, 2003, President George W. Bush honored journalists from around the world who died covering the war. In his tribute, President Bush singled out two such American reporters. Michael Kelly, of *The Atlantic*, died when the vehicle in which he was riding ran into a canal. He was the first American embedded reporter to die in the conflict. "Michael Kelly's readers," said the president, "knew of his intellectual courage. He wrote with integrity and moral

conviction, never attempting to gain favor or to please the powerful."

David Bloom was a 39-year-old reporter for NBC News. He died on April 6, from a blood clot, while reporting on the war south of Baghdad. President Bush noted Bloom's natural sincerity that people liked. "[He was] the perfect man to carry viewers along on the charge to Baghdad," said the president.

The deaths of Bloom and Kelly, along with the other reporters who died doing their jobs, are sobering reminders of the real dangers that journalists risk in bringing war news to an eager public.

LIVE

DAVID BLOOM
WITH THE THIRD INFANTRY DIV
IN IRAQ
NOW ON MSNBC.COM U.S.

NBC News correspondent David Bloom reports live from Iraq.

WEB SITES
WWW.ABDOPUB.COM

To learn more about real-time reporting, visit ABDO Publishing Company on the World Wide Web at **www.abdopub.com**. Web sites about real-time reporting are featured on our Book Links page. These links are routinely monitored and updated to provide the most current information available.

Embedded *Time* magazine reporter Robert Nickelsberg files war photographs.

TIMELINE

1861-1865
American Civil War
First photography in war coverage

1914-1918
World War I
April 13, 1917: Committee on Public Information created
June 15, 1917: Espionage Act passed
May 16, 1918: Sedition Act passed

1939-1945
World War II
December 19, 1941: Office of Censorship created
January 15, 1942: Code of Wartime Practices issued
June 13, 1942: Office of War Information created

1950-1953
Korean War

1957-1975
Vietnam War
1968: Tet Offensive
More than 100 million televisions in U.S. homes at the height
of the war

PETER ARNETT
NBC NEWS
NATE IRAQIS NATIONAL GEOGRAPHIC EXPLORER
ABOUT 150 ANTI-WAR PRO

LIVE
DAVID BLOOM
WITH THE THIRD INFANTRY DIVISION
IN IRAQ
TY NOW ON MSNBC.COM: U.S. STEPS

1980

CNN created

1991

Persian Gulf War

2001-2002

Operation Enduring Freedom

2003

Operation Iraqi Freedom
More than 500 reporters embedded with military units
64.4 million broadband Internet connections in the United States
Blogs became popular
April 27: President Bush honored journalists killed while covering
the war

Aljazeera
Exclusive

FAST FACTS

- During the American Civil War, Mathew Brady used photography to capture the first images of war.

- The press release was created during the Civil War. The military gave out fact sheets loaded with information that it wanted the public to know about.

- During World War I, the British employed only one pair of official photographers. Anyone else caught taking photos could have been sentenced to death by firing squad.

- During the peak of the Vietnam War, there were over 100 million television sets in the United States.

- During Operation Iraqi Freedom, the Pentagon allowed more than 500 members of the media to travel with coalition forces. These journalists became known as embedded reporters.

- Bryan Whitman, of the U.S. Defense Department, was the chief planner of the embedding program. The embedding program put reporters into combat units so they could cover the war live.

- The Internet has become an important tool in covering the news. During Operation Iraqi Freedom, the Nielsen/NetRatings reported that there were 64.4 million high-speed broadband connections in the United States.

- During Operation Iraqi Freedom, many people got their news on the war from Web logs, otherwise known as blogs. These blogs were on-line diaries created by individuals or groups who posted war-related news for their readers.

GLOSSARY

casualty:
A soldier or civilian who is injured or killed in an act of war.

Cold War:
The mainly diplomatic conflict waged between the United States and the former Soviet Union after World War II. The Cold War resulted in a large buildup of weapons and troops. It ended when the Soviet Union broke up in the late 1980s and early 1990s.

First Amendment:
The First Amendment to the U.S. Constitution guarantees freedom of religion, of speech, and of the press. It reads as follows: "Congress shall make no law respecting an establishment of religion, or prohibiting the free exercise thereof; or abridging the freedom of speech, or of the press; or the right of the people peaceably to assemble, and to petition the government for a redress of grievances."

Pentagon:
The large, five-sided building near Washington, D.C., where the main offices of the Department of Defense are located.

smart bomb:
A bomb or missile that navigates its way to a target, often by following a laser beam "painted" on the target by a plane or special operations soldier on the ground. Smart bombs are usually very accurate, which minimizes civilian casualties.

Tet Offensive:
In 1968, North Vietnam launched a surprise attack against American and South Vietnamese forces on the eve of the Vietnamese Lunar New Year celebration of Tet. Provincial capitals were seized, military targets attacked, and the U.S. embassy in Saigon was invaded. The offensive was costly to the North, which suffered very high casualties. But it was a media disaster for the United States, which could no longer convince the American public that it was in control of the war.

INDEX

REAL-TIME REPORTING

Learning Resources